Gilbert the Scilly Cat

by
Janice Rose.

illustrated by Yvette Wiltshire

First paperback edition printed 2020 in the United Kingdom.

A catalogue record for this book is available from the British Library.

ISBN 978-1-83853-608-4

Email: info@janicerosebooks.co.uk
www.janicerosebooks.co.uk

Published by Independent Publishing

Printed in Great Britain by Palace Printers Lostwithiel Cornwall

Gilbert
the
Scilly Cat

Here's a story I think you will enjoy. It's about the life of Gilbert, a feral cat, who was separated from his mum when he was only a few weeks old on St Martin's, an island in the Isles of Scilly. (Do you know where the Isles of Scilly are? If you look at the front of this book you will see a map of the islands, sometimes called the Scilly Isles). When you read Gilbert's story, you will learn about his adventures, travels, his catnapping and his friends.

Come and meet him.

The Rescue

Hello. My name is Gilbert, and I am a small ginger tomcat. My story started when I was about four weeks old. I was born a feral kitten, which means my cat family was living wild on St Martin's, one of the islands in the Isles of Scilly. I was left all alone by my mum. I don't know what happened to her. One minute she was there with my brothers and sisters, but when I looked around they had all disappeared. Nowhere to be seen. I thought Mum might be looking for some food for me, but she never came back. So I found a safe place to wait, hidden under a hedge. I stayed there for the rest of the night. I was petrified.

Early the next day, when everything was very still, and the sun was starting to appear, I crept out of my hiding place. I sat and wondered which way to go. I didn't know where I was, so I just started to walk. I wandered through a field. I couldn't see very much as the grass was so tall and wet from the morning dew; it made the fur on my tummy cold, soggy and heavy. I could hear a soothing noise in the near distance. I stopped and listened. It was the sea softly lapping its waves onto the beach while the seagulls flew strangely quiet overhead.

On I walked across a little pathway and got a whiff of food. It made my tummy rumble. I was starving. Following my nose, I came to the back of a large building. It was a hotel. I found some scraps of food on the floor next to the dustbins. I sniffed and greedily started to eat them. It was so nice to have some food, but chewing big pieces was difficult because my teeth were tiny.

While I was eating, two young people came walking along. Their names were Poppy and Charlie. They were chattering away and stopped and stood still when they saw me. I could see them out of the corner of my

eye, but I carried on eating because I was too hungry to stop. Poppy walked towards me and stood next to me. Her feet were bare but sparkled from sand stuck to them. She bent down, put her hand under my tummy, lifted me and began to stroke and cuddle me. Her hair was very long and fair and dangled in front of my eyes. I was so very high up and afraid she might drop me.

'He is such a tiny kitten; he must be very young. We can't leave him here,' she said. 'I'll take him back to our holiday home and see what Mum and Dad have to say.' Poppy and Charlie were cousins and away on holiday together.

Poppy's mum was sitting outside reading when she saw the kitten in Charlie's arms.

'Can we keep him?' asked Poppy.

'I don't think so,' said Mum, shaking her head. 'We live nearly three hundred miles away, and it wouldn't be fair to make him travel that far. And what would Bryher, our other cat, think?' (Bryher was named after another Scilly island.)

Poppy put me down gently, and they all stood in silence as I walked past them with my tail tucked away, curved beneath my body. I was nervous and had never been near people before. I went through a little hole in a hedge and snuggled down and went to sleep in the warm sandy soil where onions were being grown.

Everyone agreed I would need somewhere warm and dry to sleep that night. Also, that I must be a girl because I was so small and delicate. They named me Agnes after another Scilly island. How can I make them realise I'm a boy?

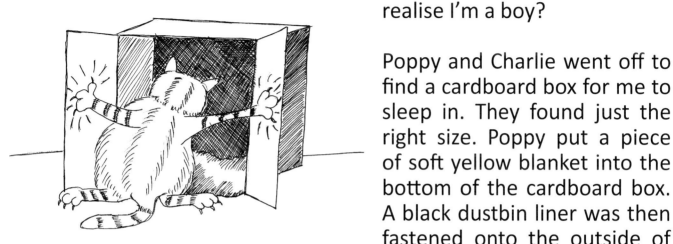

Poppy and Charlie went off to find a cardboard box for me to sleep in. They found just the right size. Poppy put a piece of soft yellow blanket into the bottom of the cardboard box. A black dustbin liner was then fastened onto the outside of the box to protect it from the wind and rain. They tried to push me in, but it was too dark inside.

I ran out and lay between the onions again. While I was hiding, I spied a little brown mouse under a bush. He was so tiny but had a very long tail; his chocolate-coloured coat was beautiful. Now, he looks a cute little fellow to play with, I thought. I watched the mouse for a few minutes busying himself dashing around. I stood up and began to walk over to him to ask if I might join in his game. He stopped in his tracks, froze and stared at me. 'What's the matter?' I asked. 'Don't you want to play?'

The mouse looked frightened and ran away. I could see his tail peeping out from behind some grass. The mouse just looked at me with panic in his eyes. 'Please don't eat me,' whispered the mouse. 'Please don't.'

'Eat you?' I replied. 'Why would I want to eat you? I only want to play. I want to be your friend.'

The mouse now looked very surprised. 'I've never heard of a cat wanting to play with a mouse before – they usually catch them and then eat them.'

'Really? Is that what I am supposed to do?' I said in surprise. My mum hadn't taught me to chase mice, so I asked, 'Can we be friends?'

'Well, I suppose so, but won't the other cats make fun of you?' asked the mouse.

'Not really,' I replied. 'I'm the only one left. My mum and brothers and sisters have gone away.'

'My name is Beanie,' said the mouse, 'because I love to eat the beans in the fields. What's yours?'

'Agnes. They think I'm a girl,' I said.

'A girl! Come on, then. I'll show you around,' said Beanie.
A little later it was starting to get dark, so Agnes and Beanie agreed to meet the next morning. As it was beginning to rain, Agnes made her way back to the cardboard box.

'There you are, Agnes. You've been gone for such a long time we thought we wouldn't see you again,' said Poppy, gently picking me up. She put me inside the cardboard box and told me to stay there for the night. Gosh, it's nice and warm in here, thought Agnes, who began to scratch and lift the blanket and found something blue and oblong but very squishy when you sat on it.

'Agnes, do you like your hot-water bottle?' Poppy asked. 'We thought it would keep you warm during the night as it's raining.'

I snuggled down and heard them tuck in the cardboard flaps on the box to keep the draught out. 'Night, night, everyone.'

It rained very hard that night and it was very foggy. A huge blaring noise made Agnes jump in her bed.

Wow! What was that? It came again – a very loud blast! It sounded four times every sixty seconds all through the night. Agnes lay very still listening to it and soon realised it was okay and felt quite safe. The loud noise was the foghorn sounding from the lighthouse on Round Island to warn ships that the rocks were very near. They wouldn't be able to see them in the fog and could crash into them. (Can you find Round Island on the map?)

The next morning was beautiful and the sun was shining. The lighthouse had done its job keeping everyone on the sea safe.
Poppy gave me some breakfast, and then I scampered off to find Beanie who was waiting for me. We played for a short while, and then I went back to my box. I felt sick.

Poppy and Charlie were quite concerned about me. Poppy asked her dad to take me to see the vet. He telephoned the vet on the island of St Mary's, who said he would meet us on the quay at St Mary's at 8:30 a.m. the following morning. We went on the boat across to St Mary's. It was a big blue boat called St Martins. It was busy with holidaymakers going home. It was carrying lots of people who had lots of luggage.

The vet was waiting. He was a large man with rosy cheeks and a warm smile. We went into the waiting room where people left their bags in between journeys. 'Let's have a look at her, then,' said the vet. He held me very gently and examined me.

I felt very ill by now and just wanted to be left alone and go to sleep.
'Well, she has got a temperature and she is a weak cat. Probably due to not having her mother around to feed her – not getting the right vitamins and all that.'
Ouch! He stuck something sharp into my bottom.
'I've given her a little injection of medicine which should make her feel better,' said the vet. He continued to examine me. 'Everything else seems okay. Just one thing… I think you need to find another name. Agnes is a boy!'

When we got back to St Martin's, Poppy's dad told everyone that I was okay but that I was quite a weak little chap.
'What do you mean "chap"?' cried Poppy.
'Agnes is a boy!' said Dad. Everyone burst out laughing, and they started to think about what my name should be.

'I know,' said Charlie, looking at a rugby ball with the make of 'Gilbert' written on it, 'we'll call him Gilbert!'

Everyone agreed it was an excellent name for an excellent kitten.
Gosh! thought Gilbert, I'd better go and find Beanie and tell him my new name now they know I'm a boy. I looked in Beanie's most favourite place; sure enough, I found him in the runner beans. 'Hi, Beanie, it's me.'

'I wondered where you'd been for the last couple of days,' said Beanie. 'I've been poorly,' replied Gilbert. 'So I went on a boat to see the vet, and he's made me better, and he told them I'm a boy! So my name isn't Agnes now; it's Gilbert!'

When I awoke the next day, I felt so much better and was very hungry. After breakfast, I went for a walk. I heard the voices of children laughing and calling to each other. It sounded like they were having lots of fun. I went to explore. I crouched down and hid and watched as the children, including Charlie and Poppy, were climbing on old fishing nets that had been strewn high in a tree. It looked a very lively game they were playing. I was fascinated and watched how they jumped and walked from one net to the other.

Later that day I went for another walk and again came to the nets. There was nobody there. All was quiet. I bet everyone is having dinner, I thought. I sat on the ground and looked up at the nets all hung and tied securely around the tree branches. I jumped up and caught my paw in the net and pulled myself up. Then I thought I would go a little higher. I was getting courageous and very proud of myself. I looked down. Oh, no! I am so high up! Then I slipped! As I began to fall, I caught both my front paws in the net, and now I was truly stuck. I didn't know what to do. I couldn't pull myself up because I had nowhere to put my back paws. I was just hanging there. My front legs were beginning to ache as I clung onto the net. What am I going to do? he thought.

Little did Gilbert know, Charlie had been watching him all the time with his hand over his mouth to stifle his giggles. He looked at Gilbert dangling, with his eyes as big as saucers and his tail sticking out as straight as a poker. 'Oh, Gilbert, what are we to do with you?' he said as he helped him down.

Oh, thank goodness I'm safe. I lay across Charlie's chest with my front paws clutching his shoulder; my heart was beating very fast. Once again, I had managed to get myself into a pickle.

The Journey Home

Life on St Martin's was excellent. I had a lovely friend, good food and a dry box to sleep in with my hot-water bottle and kind people to look after me. The sun came out every day and made everyone happy.

One day I heard Poppy's mum and dad talking about me when they were eating their breakfast. 'We can't leave Gilbert here on his own, but Bryher may be jealous if we take him home, and it's such a long way for him to travel.' After a lengthy discussion, they decided to take me home with them. I was to leave St Martin's.
I scrambled out of my box and went to find Beanie to tell him the news. I was very glum, indeed.

Poppy and Charlie found a new cardboard box for me. Holes were punched in it all around so that I could breathe easily and see outside. Then my blanket was put in for me to sleep on, and finally I was put in the box after everyone had kissed and stroked me and said their goodbyes.

My head was sticking out of the top, and I just caught sight of Beanie in the onions. I could see there were tears in his eyes. I cocked my head to one side and raised my paw. I was sorry to leave Beanie. He was such a good friend; we always had so much fun together.

Off we went. First, we had a bumpy ride on a tractor down to the quay. Then we boarded the St Martin boat again. As it left the quay, I thought

this would be the last time I would see St Martin's and where I was born. Before we knew it, we were back at St Mary's.

St Martins boat came to a stop. When I looked up, all I could see was the large white side of a vast ship. People were aboard looking down at us and waving. Poppy waved back. It was the Scillonian – the ship that sailed from Penzance to Scilly and back again every day during the summer, carrying passengers and their luggage. She was enormous.

Thank goodness we were flying back to the mainland.

We went to the airport in a taxi and boarded a light aircraft called the Skybus that only carried ten people, including the pilot. What an adventure. I have to say I was quite scared at the thought of flying. I had seen these little planes flying over Scilly every day – I never thought I would have a ride in one.

I sat in my box and said goodbye to the islands as we flew over them. Many fishing boats were sailing on the sea. Because we were high in the sky, they looked so small and still, as if they weren't moving. Then we started to descend. Bump, bump, bump. We were down and riding along the runway at Land's End. Now, that was exciting!
Before I knew it, I was in the car. Goodness me, whatever will I ride in next? I thought. Over the last two hours I had been on a tractor, a boat, a taxi, an aeroplane and now a car!

Poppy opened the top of my box and put a big strap around the outside of it. 'Well, Gilbert, are you okay? We are now back on the mainland. I'm just going to put the seat belt around your box to keep you safe.'
I curled up on my blanket and went off to sleep.

It was a long journey home. I scrambled out of my box and climbed onto the shelf in the back window of the car. Gosh, so many vehicles were travelling very fast. Every time one overtook us, I put my head down and closed my eyes very tightly. Soon, I got used to them and became intrigued with the outside world, wondering where everyone was going and where they had come from. There were big cars, little cars and huge, huge lorries and very noisy motorbikes.

It was now becoming dusk, and all the cars had turned on their headlights so that other cars could see them coming. It was getting quite difficult to see anything out of the window. The moon started to appear in the sky. The dimness was making me very tired, so I climbed back into my box and fell asleep.

Bryher and Friends

It was very dark and almost midnight when the car stopped outside the house in Manchester. Poppy lifted me from my box into the house and gently put me down. I was very nervous. Right in front of me was the most beautiful-looking grown-up cat. Ah, so this is Bryher, I thought. She was gorgeous with a dark tortoiseshell coat. She stared at me, arching her back and with the hair on her tail standing up. She looked very aggressive. Then she sat down with her body hunched looking like she was ready to pounce on me, growling all the time. She slowly waved her tail to and fro and then started to thump it loudly on the floor in anger. She was making me feel frightened. I stood and looked at her with my tail between my legs and my ears flat to my head.

'Who are you and what are you doing in my house?' she hissed.
I was lost for words and didn't know what to do.
'Now, Bryher, don't be silly,' said Poppy. 'This is Gilbert, and he is only a little kitten. He has come to live with us, and this is his home, too, so be very nice to him!' Bryher crept away.

Next morning, I was put outside in the garden. At the bottom of the garden was a large weeping willow tree, and its branches almost touched the grass. I ran to catch hold of a branch but missed and fell to the ground. I heard sniggering and looked around. Bryher was watching me, laughing. I tried again – and fell back. Bryher walked past me and very elegantly climbed the tree. I tried again and this time managed to start to climb the trunk. Wowee! I was so high up but managed to jump onto a branch. I looked down and began to wobble. Now, what am I to do? There's no way I can get down.

I sat there for ages. It was starting to get dark, and I could hear Poppy calling me. Only one thing for it. I went down backwards!

Poppy stood under the tree, laughing. 'Oh, Gilbert, you are a silly cat from the Scilly Isles.'

The following day I followed Bryher. She knew I was walking behind her because she kept stopping and sitting down, waiting for me to catch up. When I got near her, off she would go again with her tail held high as if to say 'Come on, follow me'. My legs weren't as long as hers, so it took me longer to catch up with her. Then she was gone – like a shot! She was so fast that she had vanished.

'Bryher, Bryher!' I cried. 'Where are you? Please wait for me.' I looked around; I didn't know where I was. Lots of long grass and so many trees. Bryher had already decided not to go back for Gilbert. Instead, she went home and lay in the garden in the sun. Well, that's got rid of him, she thought. Fancy trying to bring another cat here, expecting me to live with him! She went to sleep with a smile on her face.

Later that evening, Poppy went outside to call Gilbert in. She went to the willow tree and looked up. He wasn't there. 'Gilbert, Gilbert,' she shouted. She didn't get a response. Now, where on earth has he got to? she thought. Well, Bryher is here, so Gilbert must be somewhere. But there was no sign of him. Poppy went up the garden and into the fields and walked for several minutes shouting for Gilbert.

When all was quiet, I could hear Poppy shouting. I began to cry, and Poppy came to find me where I was hiding under a bush. Poppy pulled me out. I was shivering with fright and thought I had been abandoned again. Poppy carried me home and put me in my basket. Bryher crept away very sheepishly. No one would know that she had deliberately led me away. She was very jealous of me.

Gilbert soon settled down to living in Manchester but always stayed and played in the garden. He climbed trees and slept in the sun during the day and cuddled Poppy at night – and kept a very watchful eye on Bryher.

One day, Gilbert woke to an unusual noise coming from a pen in the garden. He went to investigate. 'Oh! My goodness!' I cried. 'Ducks!' There they were, two beautiful mallard ducks eating a breakfast of corn. They both had dark green heads, yellow bills and grey bodies. New friends, I thought, how we should have fun together! But I was wrong.

The ducks were called Stanley and Victor, and they hunted around the garden looking for slugs and grubs to eat. I sat in the willow tree watching them, and then I slid down the tree, backwards, and started to walk behind them, wanting to get to know them. When the ducks ignored me, I began to play a little more roughly. Their webbed feet fascinated me, so I nipped at them with my small teeth.

The ducks were not happy at all. 'Go away!' they shouted. 'That hurts.' I became more excited as I thought I had found new playmates. Because they ignored me, I jumped on Victor and tried to ride his back. These ducks are so much bigger than I am, I thought. I slid down Victor's back and wrapped my legs around his short legs, and then I fell to the ground. Humph! I tried again – but I didn't get very far.

Before I knew it, Victor was chasing me around the garden; and he wrestled me to the floor, pecking at me with his long beak. 'Stop annoying us,' said Victor.
I sat in a daze and slinked off and climbed on top of the garden shed. Bryher had watched the whole performance and sat grinning at me with satisfaction on her face.

The Catnapping

After a few months, Poppy went to visit Charlie. She took Gilbert with her. When it was time for Poppy to go home, she decided to leave Gilbert with Charlie. Charlie and Gilbert soon became good friends. Charlie would spoil Gilbert and buy his favourite food such as fish and ham, and he bought little toys for him to play with. When Charlie was out, Gilbert would busy himself in the garden walking along the top of the wall or climbing trees. He would wait for Charlie to come home and then settle down to some cuddles in the evening.

One day when Charlie came back, there was no sign of Gilbert. He went out and called his name. Still no Gilbert. Oh well, thought Charlie, maybe Gilbert has found a friend and is playing in their garden. He will come home when he is hungry.

Gilbert did not come back that night, or the next day, or even the day

after that. He had now been missing for four days. Charlie wondered where he had gone. He was anxious. He talked to the neighbours to see if they had seen Gilbert. No, they hadn't seen him for a few days. Now Charlie was distraught. He thought about what he should do next. He had an idea and wrote some leaflets about Gilbert being missing and put them through people's letterboxes.

Still no Gilbert. He put an advert in the local paper asking if anyone had seen him. No one replied. Again, no Gilbert. Charlie was desperately worried now. He was concerned that he might have wandered onto the road and been knocked down by a car. He couldn't bear to think about it.

Meanwhile, Gilbert was desperately worried, too, and afraid because he didn't know where he was. He sat and tried to remember what had happened.

I was playing in the garden and had been sitting in a tree when I saw a cat with a shiny black coat curled up asleep in a nearby garden. I thought I had found a new friend, so I climbed down from the tree and carefully and quietly walked towards the cat. The cat opened one eye and spied me coming towards him. He growled at me to go away, but I just kept on sauntering towards him. The cat stood up and arched his back, warning me not to come any nearer. He was a very grumpy cat, just like Bryher. Being a little bit afraid, I jumped onto a nearby wall and down into another garden. I wasn't sure where I was.

A young, tall, thin woman with long dark hair was in the garden hanging washing on the line. She came over to me, picked me up and stroked me and took me inside her house. She did not let me out again. I sat by the door, crying to be let out, but the door remained firmly closed. I was afraid that I might never see Charlie or Poppy or anyone else again – even Bryher! I didn't eat the food given to me; I wasn't hungry. I was very sad and terrified. I

was locked in a house with several rooms for me to wander around, but I couldn't get out.

I hadn't been outside for many days now. I just sat by the window meowing and watching people walk by. Nobody could hear me crying. Nobody came to rescue me. What is to happen to me? If I could escape, I might be able to find my way home, but I can't recognise where I am. So if I were to get out of the house, which way would I go? Should I walk down the road or up the road? Should I go around the back of the house or across the street? I just didn't know. And who was this strange woman who lived in this house and thought that I should be happy to stay with her? I am not!

I want to go home! When the woman tries to pick me up, I run away from her. When she puts food down for me, I back away and curl up in a corner feeling very sad.

Someone suggested to Charlie that he should make an announcement on the local radio about Gilbert being missing. He thought this was an excellent idea and contacted the radio station. They put out a message

asking for listeners to ring Charlie if they had seen a small ginger cat. Result! Charlie got a call from the local vicar who said he had seen a cat matching Gilbert's description in a window of a house.

Charlie went to the address the vicar gave to him. Sure enough, there was Gilbert. A young woman had seen Gilbert, thought how gorgeous he was and decided to keep him for herself. She had 'catnapped' Gilbert! Charlie was furious. He took Gilbert from the woman and carried him home. The woman started to cry and said she was sorry to have caused so much trouble.

Charlie was so relieved to have his lovely ginger cat back safe and sound, and so was I. I purred all the way home and didn't leave Charlie's side all evening, wrapping myself around his legs and jumping on his lap whenever he sat down.
Charlie fed me my favourite food of ham. Delicious.

I hurriedly ate my food and washed my face straight away.

I slept very well that night – cuddled up to Charlie in his bed!

Off We Go Again

When I was six years old, Poppy and her parents decided to move to Cornwall – near to the Scilly Isles where I was born.

Me and Bryher were put into cat boxes and loaded into the car for yet another long journey. Poppy put us side by side on the back seat.

This time we didn't get out of our boxes until we arrived at the farm where we were going to live. It was in a small hamlet with

only a few houses, but there were fields and trees everywhere. Sheep, pigs, cows, ducks, chickens, geese and bees lived there too. I was very excited to be living so close to these animals.

When I came out of my box, I scampered up a tree and sat on a branch and looked around. Well, this is very nice. There were no big roads, lots of trees to climb and inviting places to snuggle down for naps. I couldn't see any other cats around who I could be friends with apart from Bryher.

We also had a new dog called Austin who soon became my best friend. Austin and I loved living on the farm, and we explored all day long.

One day we went to see the chickens. I sat on the gate and watched Austin put his nose under the chicken house and scare a mouse out from underneath. Austin started to chase after the mouse and caught it in his mouth! I was astonished that Austin could have done such a thing.

I ran towards Austin and spat and hissed at him. 'Drop that mouse now, Austin!' Austin was so surprised at me that he dropped the mouse on the floor, and it ran away. I hissed again at Austin and stomped away. I didn't talk or play with Austin for the rest of the day. I was upset and thought of Beanie, my very first friend I'd met in the onion beds on St Martin's. I know that cats usually catch mice – I have seen Bryher do it so many times, I thought, and I was very angry with her, too.

The summer days were quite lazy days. I sat in my favourite tree most of the time watching the world go by.

One morning while I was dozing on a broad branch in the warm sunshine, I heard a strange noise and opened one eye to peer at whatever had woken me up. Who is this walking up the field? It was a massive, odd-looking bird of some kind. It had long legs and a long neck, dark feathers and a huge fan-shaped tail. The bird didn't have any feathers on his head, but there was a lot of loose skin hanging down underneath his chin. What an odd-looking bird, I thought. I sat in silence watching as the skin on its head and throat spectacularly began to change colour from red to blue – how very strange. He's making a noise that sounds like he is saying gobble, gobble. I think it's a turkey. I wonder if he needs a friend...

Back to Scilly!

The next day while I was sat cleaning myself on the kitchen windowsill, I was half listening to a conversation going on between Poppy's mum and dad. 'So everything's booked for Scilly, then?' asked Poppy's dad. 'Yes,' was the reply, 'and I've also got Scillonian tickets for Austin and Gilbert. Can't leave them behind while we go to our special place,' said Poppy's mum.

I stopped licking my paw and was completely still. Did I just hear that I am going back to Scilly? I thought to myself. Wow! How fantastic.

My tummy rolled over in that nervous sort of way it does when you're excited.

Gilbert jumped down from the windowsill, strode outside with his head held high and clambered onto his favourite branch. He went to sleep with a huge smile on his face and dreamt of seeing his first and best friend Beanie again.

The best adventure of all.

"I hope you have enjoyed reading Gilbert the Scilly Cat and heard about all his silly adventures. If you want to enjoy a little bit more of Gilbert, why not buy his colouring book and colour in all the pictures that are in the story book.

Find out more by visiting:
www.janicerosebooks.co.uk or email info@janicerosebooks.co.uk.

Cheerio for now.